RABBIT'S MORNING

NANCY TAFURI

GREENWILLOW BOOKS · NEW YORK

First Edition 10 9 8 7 6 5 4 3 2 1

Library of Congress Cataloging in Publication Data
Tafuri, Nancy. Rabbit's morning.
Summary: When the sun comes up a baby rabbit goes
exploring in the meadow and sees many other animals.
1. Children's stories, American. [1. Rabbits—Fiction.
2. Animals—Fiction. 3. Stories without words] I. Title.
PZ7.T117Rab 1985 [E] 84-10229
ISBN 0-688-04063-2 ISBN 0-688-04064-0 (lib. bdg.)

FOR MY MOTHER AND FATHER *Thank You*

The sun was hot...

karrk-
karrk

karrk-
karrk

karrk-karrk

karrk–karrk

karrk-
karrk

and rabbit came home.

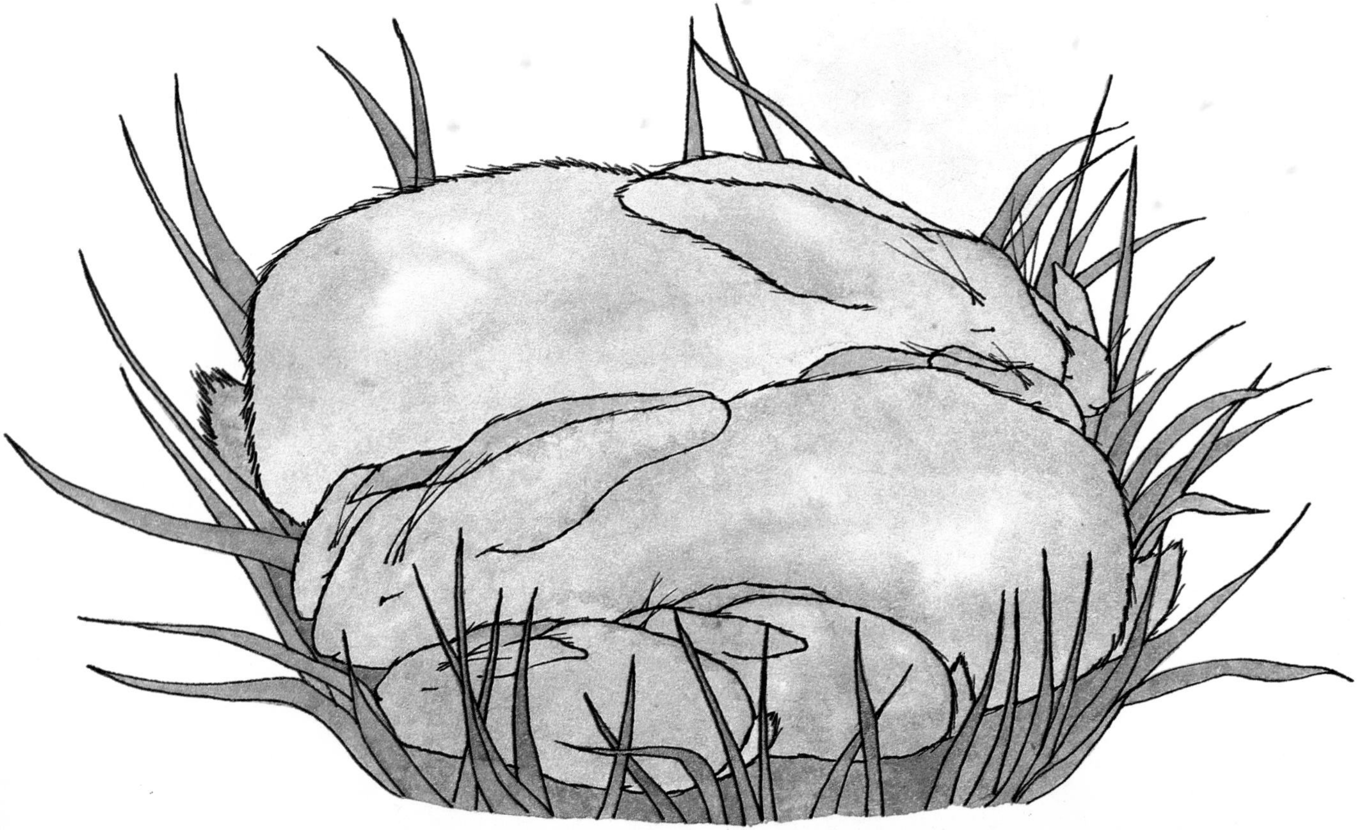